10/02.

TRACKS

GARY CREW
GREGORY ROGERS

Gareth Stevens Publishing
MILWAUKEE

Night.
Joel is hunting.

He sneaks under bushes,
He crawls through ferns . . .

Tracks!
Human tracks.

6

More tracks . . .

Mouse tracks.

Careful...
Snake tracks!

9

Strange...
Silver tracks...

What made that track?

Dog tracks,
Frog tracks.

Gnat tracks,
Bat tracks.

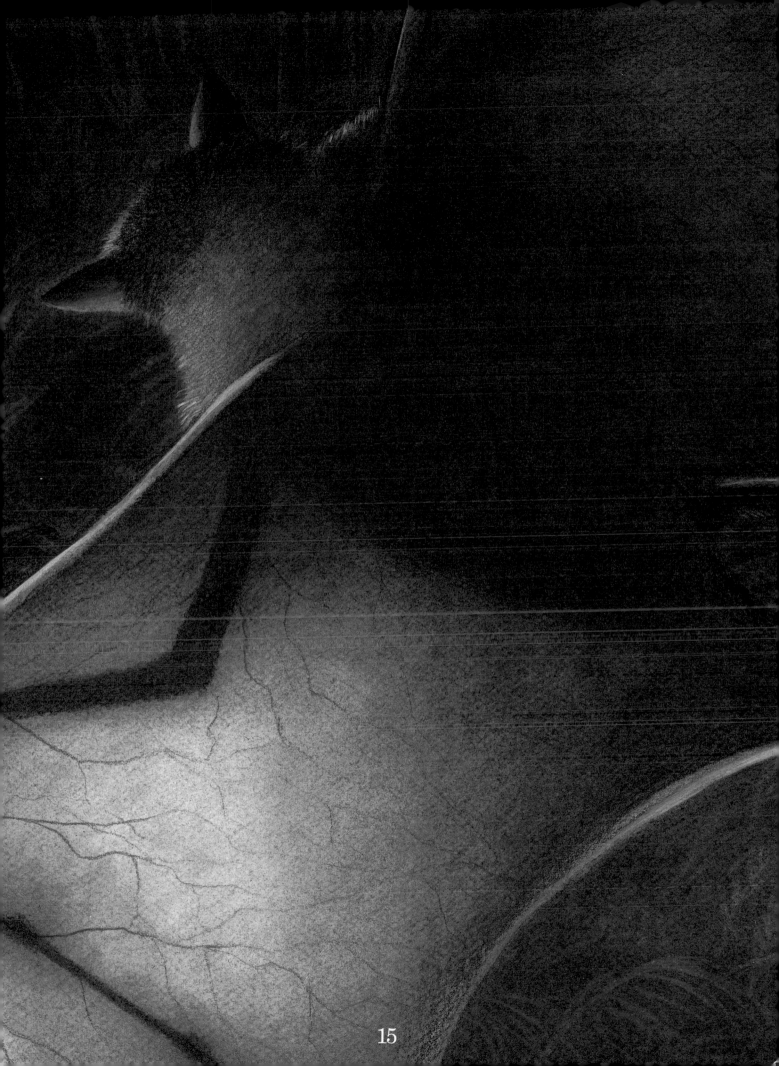

But what made that track —

That shiny silver track?

Night.
Joel is hunting.

19

He sneaks under bushes,
He crawls through ferns...

Tracks!
Owl tracks?

Fowl tracks!

Rat tracks?

Cat tracks!

That silver track again...

Follow that track . . .

Ugh! Ugly slimy slug!

**Hey! Did you make that track —
That shiny silver track?**

Wow! You're WONDERFUL!

For a free color catalog describing Gareth Stevens Publishing's list of high-quality
books and multimedia programs, call 1-800-542-2595 (USA) or 1-800-461-9120 (Canada).
Gareth Stevens Publishing's Fax: (414) 225-0377.
See our catalog, too, on the World Wide Web: http://gsinc.com

Library of Congress Cataloging-in-Publication Data

Crew, Gary, 1947-
Tracks / text by Gary Crew ; illustrated by Gregory Rogers.
p. cm. -- Summary: Joel discovers the origin of the shiny
silver tracks that he sees one night on a camping trip
and then again later in his own backyard.
ISBN 0-8368-1665-X (lib. bdg.)
[1. Slugs (Mollusks)--Fiction.] I. Rogers, Gregory, ill. II. Title.
PZ7.C867Tr   1996
[E]--dc20   96-24263

This edition first published in North America in 1996 by
Gareth Stevens Publishing
1555 North RiverCenter Drive, Suite 201
Milwaukee, Wisconsin 53212 USA

First published in 1992 by Lothian Publishing Co. Pty. Ltd., 11 Munro Street,
Port Melbourne, Victoria, 3207, Australia. Text © 1992 by Gary Crew. Illustrations
© 1992 by Gregory Rogers. Cover and text design by Gregory Rogers.

Printed in the United States of America

1 2 3 4 5 6 7 8 9 01 00 99 98 97 96